Anonymous

Boyhood

and other poems

Anonymous

Boyhood
and other poems

ISBN/EAN: 9783337367619

Printed in Europe, USA, Canada, Australia, Japan

Cover: Foto ©Andreas Hilbeck / pixelio.de

More available books at **www.hansebooks.com**

BOYHOOD

AND OTHER POEMS

BY

A. F. C.

WILLIAM BLACKWOOD AND SONS

EDINBURGH AND LONDON

MDCCCLXVIII

PREFACE.

THE poem entitled " Boyhood," and a few of the
songs in this volume, were published many years
ago by the lamented author himself. They are
now reprinted at the desire of many attached
friends, and in fulfilment of the author's own
intention, together with a small selection from
his other poems, which may not be deemed
unworthy to accompany them. And it is be-
lieved that, apart from their intrinsic merits,
they will prove no unacceptable memorial of
one who was greatly respected and esteemed
by all who knew him.

CONTENTS.

BOYHOOD

BOYHOOD.

". . . Oh that I were a child once more! . . .
Oh days of bliss!—Mansion of my fathers!—Ye vales so
green, so beautiful!—Scenes of my infant years, enjoyed by fond
enthusiasm! Will you no more return?"—SCHILLER.

I.

AWAKE, ye sweet and shadowy thoughts that bring
   Remembrance o'er me of the happy vale,
Whose rocks and woody dells were wont to ring
   With the wild glee of years I now bewail!
Ever the west wind there, with dripping wing,
   Leaving the chafed waves, the riven sail,
In its sweet glens secluded, loved to rest,
And gather softness from its peaceful breast!

II.

Lo ! shadowed forth in fancy's rising dream,
　　High from the far-seen front of Craigengower,
I view its hanging woods, its winding stream,
　　And haughty hills, on either side that lower !
Oh ! how I loved to catch day's dying gleam
　　From this same spot, in youth's unboding hour :
Now could I see it, all unheeding, sink,
For the last time, beneath the world's dark brink !

III.

Before me Carrick spreads her richest stores,
　　And Coila's plains are smiling from afar ;
Clyde, with her ample Firth, belts their bright shores,
　　While Arran's proud-shot peaks the distance bar,
Crowned with rich purple, as the toiled sun pours
　　His latest glory forth, then sinks, to war
With sleep and shadow in some other land,
And drives their dark brood to our sheltering strand.

IV.

Behind me blackening, hill o'er hill impends,
    With gloomy lakes, spilled heedlessly amid;
Monarch of all, the soaring Shalloch sends
    His hoary head aloft, by clouds half hid,
And o'er his crouching subjects frowning bends.
    Hark how the *linn's* hoarse murmur hath bestrid
The rising night-breeze, that, in fitful rush,
Breaks with its load the universal hush!

V.

But turn we to the hamlet far below,
    Its church descried through venerable trees;
And let my bosom burn with boyhood's glow
    At sight of thee—more cherished still than these—
My own paternal home! How well I know
    The fresh green beeches that my infant knees
First dared to climb—the patriarchal plane,
Whose growth my grandsires watched, as I its wane!

VI.

I mark the smoke in gladsome eddies rise—
    It tells me that the evening fire is lit;
And there may be around it brightening eyes,
    And happiness from face to face may flit;
But ah! the sweetness of the picture dies,
    With thoughts of those who once used there to sit,
Flung on the joyless world, with bosoms riven,
Or fled to reap unmeted joys—in Heaven!

VII.

Were I to enter now within the gate,
    Oh! who would wear the smile, or raise the cry,
To welcome me with bosom all elate?
    The very cattle that were wont to lie
Upon these dews, would cease to ruminate,
    And rising greet me with a steadfast eye;
But now there is no living creature there
To hail with joy the woe-worn wanderer!

VIII.

I cannot now behold my father's face,
    With placid deep affection kindling o'er :
Afar on high he hath his dwelling place,
    Where the endeared unite to part no more !
My mother bears subduing sorrow's trace,
    'Mid scenes remote from all she loved of yore :
I mourn for brothers who in promise perished,
And my sweet sisters we too dearly cherished !

IX.

Though sad, alas ! 'tis soothing to recall,
    Amid the scenes of youth, its lapsèd stream
Of joys ;—to hear remembered voices fall,
    And see long-vanished forms around us gleam :
To recognise the echo of each hall,
    And all the loved localities that teem
Upon the eager sight.   This, this might break
The callousness of hearts nought else could wake.

X.

And mine awakes once more—my thoughts afar
  'Mid perished years : what time on yon sweet holm
Each floweret, sparkling like a little star,
  Could lure me on with tottering steps to roam ;
When not a painted pebble failed to mar
  My curious path ; and every wreath of foam
That quivered on the streamlet's breast, had wiled,
But for a mother's care, her thoughtless child !

XI.

I picture me the tiny boy a-field,
  Exultingly astride his bridled cane ;
How well the urchin loves the whip to wield !
  Thou, heedless hobby ! canst not feel its pain :
But to a bolder charger thou must yield,—
  For, lo ! the house-dog trails his linkèd rein.
Ah ! happy little wight ! and can it be,
That *I* was *thou*, and *thou* must change to *me ?*

XII.

Now by the scented hedgerows, "thickening green,"
 Let us attend him in his joyous quest,
Halting where'er is wove the closest screen,
 Each tuft appearing still the wished-for nest.
Yonder, full many a Spring, the thrush unseen
  Hath reared her brood;—ah! mark her labouring
   breast
As the rude boy draws near—the painèd cry
That wrings the flutterer's bosom hovering by.

XIII.

Oft will he follow, on the "furrowed lea,"
 The cheery ploughman whistling to his team,
And strain his lip to join in symphony;
 Or from the willow that o'er-weeps the stream,
Shape the shrill pipe, and be the loudest, he.
 Long looks he for the sun's receding beam,
That, mounted on old Slowpace, he may guide,
Across the cleansing stream, and homeward ride.

XIV.

Up by the shallow rivulet he waits,
  Winding its way through broken glen and brake,
And oft his stealthy hand insinuates
  Beneath the slippery stone, intent to take
The spotted lurker ;—or, with barbèd baits,
  Casts the long line, from well-concealèd stake,
Where the broad river sleeps ;—thither the morn
On winged expectancy shall see him borne.

XV

Lo ! from the school, like eager flocks unpenned,
  A rush of happy hearts—their toil is by ;—
And to the *wiel* with flickering steps they wend :
  The bold plunge quickly in—the fearful lie
Upon the sunny brink, or shuddering send
  Half-feignèd shrieks ashore, their knees yet dry !
And *he* is there, amid the mirthful rout,
Mingling his happy voice with every shout !

XVI.

Now to the field, for sports, like swarming bees,
   The little band, with busy humming, veers ;
Some, in the volant swing, from yonder trees,
   Which Spring has clothed for twice an hundred years,
Cleave the dull air, and wake the fanning breeze ;
   Some climb the lofty trunks, scornful of fears ;
While others, timid, on the green turf lie,
And urge the adventurous as they upward ply.

XVII.

On the smooth green, or round the agèd oak,
   For future deeds their facile limbs are strung ;
Stretched in the eager race, or mimic yoke,
   Or in the heating wrestle, fiercely flung.
Now by some quickening strife their play is broke ;
   But soon anew the peal of pleasure rung ;
For with revivèd pastime peace returns,
And every heart again with transport burns.

XVIII.

Oft will they wander, till the wink of day,
  Sporting amid the mazes of the wood,
That skirts, in nature's own unconscious way,
  Yon steep that beckons to the lambent flood ;—
Or, where the monument towers o'er its grey
  Uplifted brow, from dim horizon viewed,
Hurl the cleft rock far down, with torrent leap,
And rouse the river boiling from its sleep.

XIX.

Haply, on some bright holiday they throng
  To old Blairquhan, for many a fearful tale
Of goblins famed the villagers among ;
  Lost in its woods, where nought but the hoarse wail
Of rooks can reach the ear, they learn how strong
  The mystery of loneliness !   They scale
The tottering walls to unhouse the daw, or grope
Through archways dark, that never seem to ope.

XX.

What joy is theirs, when Autumn strips the fields,
　　Sallying forth, each with his ample bag,
To cull the stores yon hanging wild-wood yields !—
　　I hear their voices echo up the crag—
And mark the reaper, as he fitful wields
　　His sickle, listening envious, idly lag :
Homeward they wend when evening shades the green,
Boasting their stocks for " hauding Hallowe'en."

XXI.

Nor does the rigid Winter all refuse
　　O'er their young pleasures to preside, but deigns
To nerve the panting bustle that pursues
　　The swiftly-bounding football, as it gains
Upon the appointed goal ; and when they lose
　　The sun, fast sinking, leads forth to the plains
The wakeful moon to light them in the race,
Or smile, sweet huntress ! on their mimic chase.

XXII.

And when the streams are wrapped in gelid sheath,
   Pleased he beholds them o'er the waters glide;
Shuddering at times to see the depth beneath
   The thin and fragile glass whereon they slide;—
Or round the *rink* among the *curlers* wreathe,
   To view the buoyant stones all stately ride;
And linger at their never-wearying play,
Till high the night is stretching on her way.

XXIII.

But in the drearest seasons of his rule,
   When sleet and snow are driving fast and cold;
The channels broad with turbid torrents full;
   When timid sheep are crouching in the fold,
And furious winds in one wild struggle pull;
   Then hold they wondering converse with the old,
Who tell of all that happened in their prime,
And rouse, or melt them, with the storied rhyme.

XXIV.

The vision fades.—Farewell! sweet vale, farewell!
  To distant scenes of care I wake once more;
But never shall my seared heart cease to swell,
  When memory's dreams thy past delights restore!
Philosophy, within her darkened cell,
  Courting vain doubts, may deem it shadowy lore
The influence of boyhood scenes to trace
On after years of life's distracting race.

XXV.

Suffice it me to have been ever led
  Through maze of gentle thought and soft desire
By the sweet haunts where erst my fancy fed;
  To have felt the first-born daring to aspire,
That from each heavenward hill, with scornful head,
  Passed to my soul, and woke its slumbering fire!—
'Mid Alps the citizen's dull blood is chill—
The mountain's son, though exiled, ardent still!

FRAGMENTS

FROM

"A RHYME ON A RAMBLE"

FRAGMENTS

FROM

"A RHYME ON A RAMBLE."

THE COAST OF AYR.

' *   *   *   *   *   *

I.

Now, let us seek the smooth and yellow shore,
   Stretching afar to hem the distant Doon;
And listen to the sea's mysterious roar,
   Blending a thousand voices in its tune—
The voices of the perished, whom it bore
   Upon its troubled breast, to whelm too soon,—
Dread Witness of God's power! we gaze on thee,
Clad in thy might, with fear,—yet cannot flee.

II.

But when, ungoaded by the furious blast,
    Thou sleepest peaceful as a wearied child,
Or on the shore thy little waves dost cast
    Gently, as if to dalliance beguiled ;
When the fierce glare of fervid noon is past,
    And o'er thy face the sunbeams wander mild ;—
While, looking to the idly flapping sail,
The wearying seaman whistles for the gale :—

III.

Then let me wander here, unmarked, alone,
    And drink the soothing influence of the scene ;
When every object round, and every tone,
    Sinks on the sense like dreams of rapture been.
Then tyrant passions from the breast are gone,
    And all within its chambers rests serene ;
While the rapt soul, as thy soft hymnings move,
Mounts to the God alike of Power and Love.

IV.

I see thy distant Castle, Greenan, cling
    Fast to the crumbling rock, where oft I've strayed
To seek the pebble.   Farther headlands fling
    Their heavy screen athwart us, and o'ershade
Princely Culzean, resting its eagle wing
    Upon the dizzy rock, secure from raid ;
And Ailsa's conic steep, that towering stands,
. Like some huge sentinel, betwixt the strands.

V.

Across the Firth I trace, distinct and high,
    The ragged ridge of Arran's rocky pile,
Majestic, mingling midway with the sky.
    Before, through sunny haze, the Holy Isle,
Lamlash, falls dun and dimly on the eye ;
    And distant Bute can scarce our sight beguile.
Near me, the Lady Isle peeps from the waters;
Beyond, the Cumrays rise, like sweet twin-daughters.

    *   *   *   *   *   *

MARGARET.

*　　*　　*　　*　　*　　*

*　　*　　*　　*　　*　　*

I.

MARGARET! And shall we pass thee o'er so lightly,
  Nor pause to give thy touching tale one tear?
Oh! no—our bosom's fire still burns too brightly,
  To think of one who might have been so dear
So coldly. Oft 'mid looks and voices sprightly,
  Thy gentle voice falls freshly on the ear
Of Memory, and thy pensive, dark, "large loving eye"
Steals on my soul's rewaking tenderly.

II.

Thou taught'st me first the power of gentleness—
  Subduèd manner—Woman's surest wile.
Thy radiant mouth told me how she can bless
  By weaving her soft witchery, a smile.
The meekness of thy filial caress
  Showed thee as Angels were in early while.
And was I then too young for love's impress?
Nay, wert thou not too sweet to view with less?

.

III.

I saw thee in thy bloom of womanhood,
  Blessing, and blessed by a declining Father,
And trod the banks, where Lugar leads his flood,
  Listening, beside thee, with delight, to gather
Sweet lessons of thy filial gratitude;
  And, in love's dawnings, fancied I would rather
Be blessed with thee in that sweet quiet glen,
Than seek for wealth or fame in haunts of men.

IV.

After some years, I had returned, and found
   Thee wed, and widowed,—weeded soon as wed.
I came upon thee, bending o'er the ground,
   To raise faint flowers, that like thy sweet self bled.
A Father's tears fell o'er thee,—for the sound
   Of thy glad voice, and radiant smile were fled.
Wed but a few short weeks—and then to part—
To part for ever !—Peace to thy poor heart !

    *   *   *   *   *

ST ANDREWS.

*　　*　　*　　*　　*

I.

Hail now St Andrews' gates of goodly span,
　Each crumbling arch telling how time hath sapped
　　　it,
And answering solemn to our steps beneath,
As if to apprise us of the City's death.

II.

Tread we the silent streets with inward awe,
　Whose spacious width of former grandeur tells,
What time our country hence proclaimed her law,
　And Rome's proud priests held men beneath their
　　　spells.

Maces and scarlet now our notice draw
  Only when Burgh Courts or College Bells
Educt the bulky Bailie, or lean student,
With paunch, or pate, prepared to let nought crude
    in 't.

III.

Erewhile upon this steep-arched causeway trod
  Full many a haughty monk in conscious power,
When hope and happiness hung on his nod,
  Making the humble crouch, the loftiest cower;
Doomed at the last to retribution's rod,
  That fails not to descend, though late the hour.
Let those who persecute the heterodox
Bethink them of the spirit of John Knox!

IV.

Mark ye yon crumbling towers and ragged wall,
  Where the rank weed in mockery creeps around;—
At sunset there the priest, in gorgeous pall,
  Paced the majestic nave, to vespers bound.

The morrow's sun beheld its glory fall,
　　Dragged to the ground, of stones a shapeless
　　　　mound !
What scarce thrice fifty years of labour formed,
A single day of deep-roused vengeance stormed.

V.

There, on the right, within that lengthened hall,
　　Where erst our Scottish Parliament did meet,
Look in,—some grave professor, at the call
　　Of daily news, is glancing o'er a sheet
Of Scotch economy, from Hume or Maule,
　　In Parliament's now far translated seat ;
While round him thickly rank departed sages,
That long to shake the dust from off their pages.

VI.

Wending our way where crowds were wont to throng,
　　The very children mark that we are strangers,
And stop their sports to see us pass along ;
　　And we encounter now and then some dangers,

As passing sylphs suspend the tripping tongue,
　　And send a quick yet soft glance on the rangers.
When gone, I hear a gently rising flutter;
But can't exactly tell you what they utter.

VII.

Some fifteen centuries have wreaked their storms
　　On the square ribs of that high Pictish tower;
And yet its scarless unworn vigour forms
　　A rare example of Time's baffled power.
Nor is it Nature round yon castle worms:
　　There scornful Beatoun, in an impious hour,
Viewed from its windows Wishart's martyrdom.
The walls tell guilt—its hour will surely come!

VIII.

Let us descend this dizzy crumbling brow,
　　With careful step, to see St Rule's bleak cave;—
Though rude neglect scarce leaves us access now.
　　In safety here he bade the ocean rave,

And the fierce winds with all their fury blow;
 While he, unheeding, Heaven's help would crave,—
His altar rude hewn from the living stone,—
Or rest within, lulled by their ceaseless moan.

IX.

Once more above let us send forth our gaze
 Across the bay, and view Arbroath's brown shores.
Far off, their lofty brows the Grampians raise;
 Nearer, the Tay its ample deluge pours;
While thither labouring prows direct their ways,
 And leaping waves would fain be at their stores.
Delay not there 'mid rocks and shoals, but flee,—
Else there may be sad wailing at Dundee.

X.

Disastrous bay! the elements delight
 To hold their boisterous revels on thy breast,
And fling aloft the billows riven, white,
 Baring thy tenants in their secret rest.

In vain the feeble bark vies with their might,
 'Mid hidden sands, and many an ambushed crest,
Darting, as sea-mew swift, before the gale,
Till suddenly " they strike, and all is wail !"

XI.

I can remember well a harassed sail,—
 It is some dozen years since,—in its flight,
Rushed on the shoals, where Eden seemed to hail ;
 And the whole city hurried at the sight,
Along yon westward sands, in straggling trail,
 To witness or relieve the seamen's plight,—
Dragging the lifeboat swift along the shore,
And drowning with their shouts the Ocean's roar.

XII.

The ship's tight yawl and crew had reached the strand,
 But left one little cabin-boy behind.
We could descry him looking to the land—
 Perhaps upbraiding mates he deemed unkind.

What now his thoughts? The safety-boat is manned,
　　Now tacking round, now facing waves and wind,—
Receding oft, yet gaining by degrees—
Borne like a bladder on the heaving seas.

XIII.

'Tis now so near, it seems as he might leap
　　Into its welcome bosom,—lo ! again,
The fierce upheaving swell, with one fell sweep,
　'Dashing it back, renews his deathlike pain.
But now, 'tis reached—he's safe—and o'er the deep
　　With buoyant course the shore they quickly gain;
While eager crowds close round the rescued boy—
And *he*—but who could paint *his* inward joy?

XIV.

Fit spot were this to rouse the soul to deeds,
　　Fierce, and as bold as th' elemental rage.
The winds, the waves, each rock with fury feeds,
　　Like the stern warrior's, rushing to engage.

Lo ! where the heavy gathering billow leads
 His lengthened troop inflexible to wage
Dread combat with the firm and mailèd rock,
While earth far inward reels beneath the shock !

  *   *   *   *   *   *

MY FATHER'S DEATH.

.*   *   *   *   *   *

I.

O ! THOU, my Father, numbered with the blest,—
    Why do I thus call up thy vanished form,—
Waking again within our sorrowing breast
    The wounds, not recent, but alas ! yet warm ?
Strange ! that the human heart should cherish best
    The memory of grief.   Not pleasure's charm
Thrills us long after, as doth sorrow stealing
O'er the deep chords of sad responsive feeling.

II.

Of all the countless springs of mortal grief
    Can aught e'er crush us like a Father's death ?—
The death of such as thou?—Tempered and brief—
    Compared—a brother's—sister's parting breath ;

For these, though oft too slowly, comes relief,
　And, if connubial—filial—wrecks bequeath
Grief as intense,—ere such can overwhelm,
Submission sits with Reason at the helm.

III.

But, when a Father whom his children love,
　And loving fear not, perishes,—ere yet
Aught from without their charmèd circle move
　The heart's affections,—youth's high dreams are set.
He whom their thoughts had imaged nought above—
　In whom protection, love, instruction met,—
With whom the very world itself seemed blent!
A new life dawns,—but ah! how different!

IV.

Oh! with what heavy hearts they gather round
　The ever blissful hearth till now;—for where
Is *his* calm smile paternal, that still bound
　Affection in its wreath? While blank despair

Dries up their speech, they listen for the sound
   That wont to issue from his vacant chair,
And oft his name, recurring unawares,
Starts the quick tear amid their nightly prayers.

V.

Undying still—oh ! never doomed to fade
   In memory's shrine, dwell the last fleeting days,
When fearful, watching, feebly we essayed
   To pay a life of love.   With painful gaze
Marking thy trembling frame, the pallid shade
   That settled on thy cheek,—thine eye's dim rays,
Calm and resigned, although regretful, cast
On us who saw thy life was ebbing fast.

VI.

The last dread night, when, Heaven's high will fulfilled,
   Thy spirit to its blessed Redeemer rose,
And to our listening ears thy breath was stilled.—
   Then knew we 'twas indeed thy long repose !

Near yonder ruined fane, where thou hadst willed,
  The crumbling walls thy relics now enclose,
By thy loved Daughter's side,—to be with whom
Thou almost bad'st a welcome to the tomb.

*   *   *   *   *   *

MISCELLANEOUS POEMS

MISCELLANEOUS POEMS.

THE LOVES OF ECHO.

I.

The Day calls in his wearied beams,
　　And Echo sleeps in rocky chambers;—
Of Sound the gentle dotard dreams,
　　While love-lorn Silence guards her slumbers.

II.

Sweet Nymph of rocks and haunted streams,
　　Soft be thy sleep, and fresh thy waking!
At morn again, like fitful gleams
　　Of Memory, around us breaking.

III.

List ! from the shallows of the rill,
   Half-stifled by the young waves' kisses,
In many a struggling syllable,
   How Sound is chiding their caresses !

IV.

And now to Echo's couch he creeps,
   With her light dreams his voice is blending;
Hark ! her fond murmurs as she sleeps—
   Poor Silence flees—his heart is rending.

V.

The goodly Day is forth again,
   And jocundly young Sound is singing;
He loves to swell the Shepherd's strain
   Or Reaper's laugh, when Mirth is winging.

VI.

He wakes the woodland minstrel's lay—
   The house-dog's happy chorus blending,—
Treads, with the flock, the dizzy way,—
   Or cheers the herd o'er meadows wending.

VII.

Where'er his path, rapt Echo still,
   Like Passion's self unbodied, follows,—
Skips, fancy-footed, o'er the hill,
   Or skims the vales and shady hollows.

VIII.

Stung at their loves, lorn Silence sighed,
   And burst his charmèd link of being;
Yet his lone spirit loves to glide
   To Echo's cell, when day is fleeing.

SONG.*

I.

I SIGH for Night's sweet coming,
    For the hour that brings me thee—
The gentle hour of gloaming,
    When the leaf sleeps on the tree;
When the streams have raised their voices,
    And the floweret closed its breast,
And the weary earth rejoices
    At the balmy hour of rest.

II.

I watch the Sun's receding,
    And the Evening's starry birth,
And I steal to thy soft pleading,
    The happiest thing on earth.

* Set to music by W. Patten.

I see the Moon awaking,

On the cloud's soft breast recline,

While my heart is almost breaking,

To press thee unto mine.

ANACREONTIC.

I.

When a downy-chinned stripling,
I began my sad tippling,—
Oh ! woman's glance, then, was my nectar,
So brilliantly streaming,
Like Heaven's light gleaming.
When love and youth's loveliness decked her.

II.

But since Age now has dried me,
Such potion's denied me,
For the girls, laughing, point to my wrinkles ;—
Yet there is not a furrow
Left among them by sorrow,
And my path rosy Pleasure still sprinkles.

III.

For I laugh 'mid my quaffing,
And quaff 'mid my laughing,
And my halls ring the praise of old Bacchus;
Let Care come—the fellow
Himself we'll make mellow,
Nor dread that he then will attack us.

IV.

Such old men as I am,
'Mid the troubles that try 'em,
Can quaff, and think grumbling is folly;
Should e'en Time with *his* glass come,
We'd fill it and ask him
To taste what it is to be jolly.

ADDRESS TO THE GREEKS.

WRITTEN IN MARCH 1823.

I.

On ! comrades to the work !
See ! battle woos the brave, the free :
Strike, Hellenists, for liberty,—
    For vengeance on the Turk !
      Tyrants accursed !
The earth they tread indignant throbs,
That yet unsmote the Moslem robs
    The sons she should alone have nursed.
    The dastard stain departs !
We breathe unchained, or cease to breathe ;—
Till then our swords shall know no sheath
    But Turkish hearts !

II.

Is there a recreant thought
Can steal its way 'mid struggling throngs.
That tell the foul, the goading wrongs
  The Mussulman hath wrought?
  The wives we clasp,
Our brides and our betrothed are torn,
To feed his low-born lust, or scorn,—
  To writhe in his polluting grasp.
  Spirits yet unavenged
Shriek havoc on the murderous foe ;-
Vengeance responds not slack or slow,—
  Else Greece *is* changed !

III.

Think on Thermopylæ !
Sons of the sires whom Marathon
Embraced in deathless burial,—on !
  Be bold, be free as they !

Think on the shame
That lawless Turks should lording dwell,
Where countless Persians fled or fell,
    And wrapped our land in glory's flame !
    Think how she ruled the world !
Then view th' unhallowed Crescent gleam,
Where Freedom's sacred flag should stream
    To heaven unfurled !

IV.

Forward ! be Greeks ! be men !
Greece is no more the Moslem's spoil !
The fruit of Freedom's natal soil
    Is liberty again !
    Our shame efface !
Grasp we the sword, and snatch the brand,
To purge from our polluted land
    All vestige of the hated race,—
    The race our blood imbues !
On ! let their ships be funeral pyres !
'Twixt hungering seas and gorging fires,
    The Turk may choose !

HYMN FOR MY CHILDREN.

'Twas God who made this glorious world—
　The starry heavens—the smiling earth;
The mountains high He upward hurled;
　He poured the ocean's waters forth.

He filled with life the lonely woods,—
　The fields with flowers and verdure decked,—
Gave sea and air their sportive broods,—
　And, king o'er all, man walked erect.

But man himself was made by God;
　He breathed not till th' Almighty spoke.
God formed him of the humble sod,—
　And with a soul the clay awoke!

D

Albeit man return to earth,
  The kindred earth from which he rose ;
Yet we shall wake in second birth,
  With blessed lives that never close.

For though this weak flesh cannot last,
  The soul that fires it never dies,
But dwells, when life's short span is past,
  In purer frame above the skies.

Yes ! there are pleasures evermore
  For all the good beyond the grave.
Oh ! let us then God's name adore,
  And seek His grace our souls to save.

SONNET:

ON A HAREBELL BROKEN BY THE WIND.*

SWEET harebell! beautiful as heaven's own smile,
　And delicate as aught that dwells on earth ;
Why was such sweetness doomed so short a while
　To deck the turf that proudly gave it birth ?
I saw thee 'neath the gently stirring air
　Avert thy head and bend thy slender form,—
As when a modest, young, and timid fair
　Shrinks from the gaze unconsciously too warm.
Methought I should revisit thee full oft,
　And see thee blooming while the summer smiled :
Alas ! the winds spared not a flower so soft,
　But robbed the parent sod of its sweet child !
'Tis thus the gentle feel the storms of life ;
The stubborn only can resist their strife.

* This and the four following poems were written in early
youth.

SONNET:

TO THE FLOWER FORGET-ME-NOT.

" Forget me not !" thou say'st, soft gentle thing,
  Miniature of woman's heaven-reflecting eye !
Who once hath paused to see thee blossoming,
  Will not forget, or heedless glide thee by.
Sweet little sapphire, sparkling on the breast
  Of jewelled meads, 'mid other gems of spring;
Not every skimming glance thy rays arrest,
  Passing to those that gaudier colours fling;
But when thou meet'st the more inquiring gaze,
  'Twill linger tasteful o'er thy simple charms.
And scorn for thee the meretricious blaze
  Of glittering hues and more obtruding forms !
True beauty thus, once seen, is ever sought;
And glare, and art, and show beheld as naught.

THE VIOLET.

I.

How sweetly blows yon violet,
  Within its low retreat!
There springs no fairer floweret;
  None scents the air so sweet.
Yet modestly. beneath the shade.
  It lurks retired from view!
Nor courts the wanderer in the glade
  To mark its beauteous hue!

II.

So blooms my Anna's youthful form,
  So soft, so sweet, so fair!
Though every eye its graces charm,
  What modesty is there!

The crystal drop upon that flower
Is not more pure than she !
Less dear to it the vernal shower
Than her soft smile to me !

A FAREWELL.

FAREWELL to the valley where Girvan winds sweetly,
   With green sloping banks, round each wild-woody
     hill !
Within its loved bosom the moments passed fleetly ;
   Though fled, I will cherish their memory still.

Sweet scene of my youth, where in gladness I've
     sported,
   Amid the wild dells through the long summer day ;
With fondness I'll think upon thee, when we're parted,
   And still thou'lt be dear when I'm far, far away.

Farewell to my comrades that dwell in yon hamlet,
   Who with me through all my fond haunts oft have
     strayed ;

The hills we have climbed,—we have laved in the
  streamlet,—
  Together we've wandered through woodland and
  glade.

How happy with them were my hours in the valley !
  I ne'er can forget them wherever I roam.
And when I'm far distant, my bosom will swell aye.
  So oft as I think of my earliest home !

A LAMENT.

My Jamie's left our peacefu' glen,
Ah ! never to return again !
I waefu' wander noo alane
    Through greenwood shaw,
To think on joys for ever gane,
    Since he's awa'.

When bairnies, trotting o'er the lea,
In careless play and giddy glee,
The birds that sang on ilka tree,
    Sae simply sweet,
Were never half sae blithe as we,
    On lightsome feet.

An', whan we grew, my daily joy
Was wanderin' wi' my shepherd boy,
To weary out in youthfu' ploy
    The summer sun,
Nor think ought could our bliss destroy,
    Till life was done.

The flowery turf in mony a dell
Our youthfu' lingerin' haunts can tell,
Whare scented thyme and heather-bell,
    An' violet,
That loves in lanely shade to dwell,
    Langsyne we set.

Whiles we wad sit upon the brae,
To see the little lammies play;
Whiles by the wimplin' burnie stray,
    Or roarin' linn,
To wonder at the dashin' spray,
    An' ceaseless din.

Whiles up the hangin' rock we'd creep,
To see the stane, wi' torrent leap,
Frae crag to crag shoot down the steep,
    Till loud it splashed,
As, rushin' headlong, in the deep,
    Dark wiel it dashed.

How fleetly then the moments went.
As thus the simmer day we spent!
An' whan the sun his crimson lent
    To robe the West,
Our wearied feet we hameward bent,
    To peacefu' rest.

But now our joys are turned to waes,
For far awa' my Jamie gaes,
An' bravely meets his country's faes,
    To battle rushin',
Whare glitterin' swords around him blaze,
    An' bluid is gushin'.

An' maybe there he's doomed to dee,
Far, far frae a' his friends an' me,
Wi' no a ane to close his e'e,
        Or soothe his pain ;
An' oh ! this life, what wad it be,
        If he were gane ?

Why, Jamie, didst thou leave our glen,
Ah ! never to return again !
Why must I wander now alane
        Through greenwood shaw,
To think on joys for ever gane
        Wi' thee awa' ?

IMITATION OF AN OLD SONG.

I.

OH ! were my love yon violet,
  That sighs beneath the shading thorn ;
And I the wildered breeze that walks
  Upon the balmy face of Morn ;
How would I lingering love to rest,
  Pillowed near on the trancèd brook,
And ope to kiss its gentle breast,
  Where Heaven itself may scarcely look !

II.

Or, were she yon Narcissus fair,
  That all impassioned hangs its head ;
And I the Spirit of the air,
  That called it from its wintery bed ;—

It should not feel the sickening breath,

    That Summer's languid breezes bring,—

Nor Autumn's throes,— nor Winter's death,—

    But bloom in undeparting Spring!

KILRULE.*

THOUGH rude be thy rocks, the wild waves dashing
    round,
  While the lone caves reply to their hoarse meas-
    ured roar ;
.Yet I love thee, Kilrule, for thy bleak walls surround
  The friends that I love and the girl I adore.

Thy dark frowning cliffs appear smiling to me,
  When I think that those friends are oft wandering
    above,
.And thy boisterous billows a smooth swelling sea,
  When their spray sprinkles softly on her that I
    love.

* St Andrews.—See Notes to Scott's ' Marmion.'

E'en the blast, as it rudely embraces her form,
   And blends with her breath, of its fury beguiled,
No longer appears as the breath of the storm,
   But, sharing *her* softness, sighs gently and mild.

The strand where rich verdure and forests abound
   May be lovelier deemed than thy bold naked shore;
But I love thee, Kilrule, for thy bleak walls surround
   The friends that I love and the girl I adore.

— —

PRINTED BY WILLIAM BLACKWOOD AND SONS, EDINBURGH.

www.ingramcontent.com/pod-product-compliance
Lightning Source LLC
Chambersburg PA
CBHW030026030726
47499CB00008B/3134